Dear Parent:
Your child's love of reading starts here!

Every child learns to read in a different way and at his or her own speed. Some go back and forth between reading levels and read favorite books again and again. Others read through each level in order. You can help your young reader improve and become more confident by encouraging his or her own interests and abilities. From books your child reads with you to the first books he or she reads alone, there are I Can Read Books for every stage of reading:

SHARED READING
Basic language, word repetition, and whimsical illustrations, ideal for sharing with your emergent reader

BEGINNING READING
Short sentences, familiar words, and simple concepts for children eager to read on their own

READING WITH HELP
Engaging stories, longer sentences, and language play for developing readers

READING ALONE
Complex plots, challenging vocabulary, and high-interest topics for the independent reader

ADVANCED READING
Short paragraphs, chapters, and exciting themes for the perfect bridge to chapter books

I Can Read Books have introduced children to the joy of reading since 1957. Featuring award-winning authors and illustrators and a fabulous cast of beloved characters, I Can Read Books set the standard for beginning readers.

A lifetime of discovery begins with the magical words **"I Can Read!"**

Visit www.icanread.com for information on enriching your child's reading experience.

LIBRARY

READ TO

For Elliot Jude Chaplin,
and for our beloved librarian
friends who share the love of
reading with all of us!
—A.S.C. and P.S.

For information address HarperCollins Children's Books, a division of HarperCollins Publishers, 10 East 53rd Street, New York, NY 10022. www.icanread.com

ISBN 978-0-06-193507-7 (trade bdg.) — ISBN 978-0-06-193506-0 (pbk.)

14 15 16 17 18 LP/WOR 10 9 8 7 6 5 4 3 2 1 ❖ First Edition

Biscuit Loves the Library

story by ALYSSA SATIN CAPUCILLI
pictures by PAT SCHORIES

HARPER
An Imprint of HarperCollins*Publishers*

It's a very special day
at the library, Biscuit.
Woof, woof!

READ
TO A
PET DAY!

It’s Read to a Pet Day!

I can read to you,

Biscuit.

Woof, woof!

Come along, Biscuit.
Let's find a book.
Woof, woof!

See, Biscuit?

There are books

about bunnies and bears.

Woof, woof!

And big dinosaurs, too!

Woof!

Funny puppy!

That's not a real bone!

Woof, woof!

Look, Biscuit.
There are more books
over here.
Woof, woof!

Biscuit! Where are you?

Woof!

You found the puppets,
Biscuit.

Woof, woof!
And you even found
stories we can listen to.
Woof!

Now, which book will it be?

Woof, woof!

Biscuit! Wait for me!

Woof!

Oh, Biscuit!

You found the librarian
and a book that's just right.
Woof, woof!

You found a cozy spot
filled with friends, too.

Everyone loves the library,
Biscuit.
Woof, woof!

Let's read!

Woof!

LIBRARY